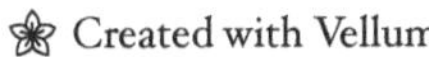 Created with Vellum

A DOCTOR'S TOUCH

An Erotic Queer Novella

RAM SKIN SERIES

A. A. FAIRVIEW

Praise for A Doctor's Touch

"For all the vampire and werewolf lovers out there, A.A. Fairview's *A Doctor's Touch* simmers with sizzling and tender eroticism."

— MORGAN DANTE, AUTHOR OF A FLAME
IN THE NIGHT

The atmosphere *A Doctor's Touch* feels like wrapping oneself in a warm blanket before settling in to read a cherished murder mystery. Set in a sleepy forest town, this tender but thrilling erotic romance touches on trans joy, sexual exploration, and the sometimes blood-stained lengths we'll go to protect those we love. Fairview carefully balances sharpened tension with quiet domesticity and light humor, perfect for readers who enjoy familiar banter between two old souls who've finally found true acceptance within each other. - Elle Porter author of Hyacinth.

— ELLE PORTER AUTHOR OF HYACINTH

Content

A Doctor's Touch is an erotic romance with a trans man narrator. The love interest is a cis man.

Possible triggers - Violence, gun violence, reference to suicide, murder, blood, references to antiquated medical practices.

This story is sexually explicit and contains - knotting, anal & vaginal sex, blood play, face sitting, face fucking, rimjob.

A Doctor's Touch previously lived as a newsletter magnet, it has since been expanded upon and re-edited for this publication.

Here speaks a citizen, a servant of people. May I be destroyed if I betray these words.

— HIPPOCRATES' OATH AS TRANSLATED BY
AMELIA ARENAS.

A Doctor's Touch

THE LAST PLACE I EXPECTED TO SEE CAMRON COININ WAS on my front stoop. Let alone at three AM holding a bloody wound. Though lucky for him he stumbled to my abode. I didn't sleep. Hadn't for a century. Camron gurgled his words, struggling to stay upright. Shirtless, I could see his chest hair was matted with blood, as were his jeans. He held onto his right side. Stepping out of my house meant possibly running into whatever had attacked him. I was sure the Hippocratic oath didn't demand doctors put themselves at risk before a patient.

But I stepped outside. I wrapped one of his massive arms around my shoulder and then struggled to hold onto his waist. Not only was he slippery with blood but Camron was one of those men that was big all over. Big shoulders, big stomach, big head... We made it a few steps into my cabin before Camron fell to his knee, taking me with him. Blood dripped onto the linoleum floor of my kitchen.

"I'm calling the office," I told him. There weren't any ambulances in our little town hidden in the woods. If there was something dire our clinic couldn't handle, the best bet for a patient's survival was an airlift. Dramatic? Yes. But when it would take two hours for an ambulance to even reach the edge of the woods, what else were we supposed to do? Dramatic was better than dead.

I stood only halfway up before Camron grabbed my wrist with a strength I didn't expect from a man bleeding out. "Don't—" he coughed. "Don't call nobody..." My eyes went wide but that had little to do with Camron's words. I could see them now, his claws wrapped around my arm. Black and curved and sharp as hell. As Camron struggled to breathe I peered into his mouth and saw his elongated canines. I looked up, the curtains on my kitchen window open to the night. The full moon peered past some clouds.

"Camron," I spoke sternly, having accepted that I was now on the clock. "Camron, stay with me, I need to ask you some questions."

"I got shot."

"Shit," I cursed, already failing to be the cool-headed person in the room. "Stay here."

I rushed to the closet to grab my emergency kit. It was much heftier than the average first aid kit you could get anyplace. Rural medicine required a lot of work outside the office space. Some, most I'd dare to say, found the lack of resources stressful. I found it familiar. A return to a time before penicillin or even peroxide.

I returned to Camron's side, reaching for his neck to check his pulse, obvious tachycardia. At least his breathing was still slow. Camron's one hand still clung to his wound. "I need to examine the injury," I told him. I reached for his hand to move it aside, only to find he had dug his claws into his flesh, like a panicked cat clinging to its owner. "Damn it," I breathed. I started to pull his claws out one digit at a time till finally I could get at the injury.

Camron muttered, "I got shot..."

I huffed, happy he could talk even if he was repeating himself. Doing what he always did as the site manager— the bull of the woods at the lumber yard in town. He came into the clinic at least once a week, accompanying some injured worker from the site. I always tried to get him to talk to one of the nurses. Hell, even the secretary— because anytime he talked to me he acted so stiff, his heavy brow made heavier by his frown. I hadn't a clue as to why he hated me.

I'd accepted he disliked me for whatever reason. I might have been only one of two doctors in town but my status didn't stop the gossip. Being single always had people wondering. I kept to myself. Then there were the things I couldn't even control. Every time a fear-mongering news anchor warned about medicine— the very thing that could have saved so many were it only available sooner, there were extra eyes on me. I made it worse by offering HRT therapy. My only regret was my own expectations. I didn't think so many people would travel so far to try and speak with me. It was worth it, sure, but now I had patients all across the state.

In all my 200 years I'd never been so stressed.

And that was before the arrival of a werewolf, bleeding out in my kitchen.

I reached up onto my kitchen counter and managed to grab a wooden spoon. It had never been used, a prop in my never-ending act of humanity. "Bite down," I ordered Camron as I shoved the spoon in his mouth. It really was just like old times, though thankfully I didn't have to saw off any infected limbs. No... just fishing a bullet out of this poor man's gut. To Camron's credit he didn't flinch when I dipped my forceps into his wound. Though I could hear the wood splintering against his teeth.

I fished the bullet out. The work had just begun but the bullet gave me pause. In the yellow light of the kitchen, it reflected white. A silver bullet. I looked down at Camron, his face drenched with sweat and a half-broken spoon in his mouth. There was little doubt in my mind up to that point that he was a werewolf, but the bullet confirmed it.

And also confirmed that someone was hunting him.

As much as I wanted to run and lock my door, I knew Camron would only start to lose more blood now that the injury was open. "Take deep breaths through your nose." There wasn't any time to numb the injury. I'd have to stitch him up as-is. It was a long night ahead, yet I feared the morning more.

"Hilliary? Yes, I'm sorry, I have to call out today..." The curtains were all drawn in my cabin, though the sun wouldn't rise for another hour or so. I had the clinic's secretary on the phone and Camron in my bed. Again, the bed was just a prop. I wasn't even sure if it was all that comfortable, but Camron had managed to fall asleep anyway, lying on top of the tight covers. "If there's an emergency, do call me, okay? I'll find some way to come in." She was understanding but I hated leaving the clinic in a lurch like this.

I hung up the landline and went to check on my patient, guiding my fingers to his neck. Pulse was normal. He *should* need a blood transfusion but I heard werewolves healed fast. Now that the silver was out of his system, I thought he should be fine in a day or two. Unless the silver had found a way into his bloodstream. What could I have possibly known? I worked on humans; not werewolves, not vampires.

I shamelessly looked over Camron's body. Once he was stable I took the time to wash the blood from his chest with a washcloth and warm water. He had a little pudge, a "dad-bod" as I've heard it affectionately referred to. But he still had muscle, which made sense for a tree climber. Even though he was the boss, he still rigged himself up, climbing fifty feet in the air to trim branches before cutting. I could never. I liked my feet on the ground, thank you very much—despite my association with bats.

The hair on Camron's chest was darker than the blonde on his head. Did the carpet match the drapes? I wouldn't dare look, even when his pants were completely soiled. I doubted they were very comfortable at the moment but I couldn't change him without risking opening his wound. That and he had a good fifty pounds on me.

Camron stirred and I jumped, embarrassed to be caught staring. Though he was much too groggy to notice. His eyes fluttered open. I'd never looked too close to his eyes. Admittedly, I usually only peered at him over my charts at work and his eyes were always shadowed by his brow. But his eyes were blue. A lovely shade like the sky over the plains in the summertime, a sight I hadn't witnessed since I was turned.

He let out a heavy sigh, his chest rumbled. "Hey, Doc..."

I wished I had a clipboard to hide behind right now. "How are you feeling?"

"Like I stood too close to a powder wedge and got blasted."

I just nodded. Though I wanted to ask him what happened, it felt like lying. I knew, approximately, what had happened. Camron went out for the full moon, as all werewolves do, and he was unlucky enough to cross paths with a hunter. Except this hunter knew full well what they were hunting. Which was bad. For the both of us.

I licked my lips and gathered my courage. "Camron—"

"Doc," he interrupted. We both looked at each other, faces blank. Then a grin tugged at Camron's lips, showing off a dimple on his left cheek beneath his short stubble. "You keep my secret and I'll keep yours?"

"Excuse me?" I managed to remain calm despite the werewolf in my bed blackmailing me. If that was what he was doing.

"I know what you are, Doc. I've known since we've met."

If I had the ability to sweat I would have right through my shirt. I realized my mouth was hanging open, like the mounted bass proudly displayed in every neighbor's cabin. I licked my lips once more. "How?"

"You smell different. Not bad, just different."

I was grateful he'd clarified. Being half dead, I would worry I smelled like a corpse. Nowadays most people associated the dead with the smell of formaldehyde. I, however, knew all too well what a body smelled like when it had been left to rot.

My silence must have bothered Camron because he clarified further. "Other people, I can smell their blood. Coppery, right?"

"Not for me." Never did I think I'd be discussing blood drinking with anyone. "I wouldn't say blood tastes very metallic to me."

Camron hummed. "Point is, you don't have that smell. There's no blood in your veins is there?"

"No," I confirmed. "No, I'm a shambling corpse, essentially."

"Look pretty good for a corpse," Camron replied.

I told myself this wasn't flirting even if it felt like it. He was being cordial because I'd saved his life. The reminder to myself pinged another reminder, to get to the bottom of what had happened. "Camron, did you see who shot you?"

He shook his head and I could see his jaw tighten. "Fucker had a hat on and no safety vest. I didn't see him till he had his sights lined up. I saw one eye. He had a cowl on too."

"He knew what he was doing..." I mused aloud. "But it sounds like it was just one person?" I inquired. "No one is foolish enough to hunt in the dark with a partner but without a vest."

"No one is dumb enough to hunt werewolves," he pointed out. "But there are idiots abound I guess..."

I shook my head. "We need to figure out who could know what you are."

"We?"

"Yes, *we*. If this person is going after you I could be next. I know it pains you to work with me—"

"What gave you that impression?" He looked genuinely confused.

I frowned, thinking back to all our chats at the infirmary. Maybe he looked at me with disdain because of my smell. A vampire moonlighting as a human doctor did sound shady. But I took my oath seriously. I rarely, if ever, drank from live bodies. Blood infusions were only good for 42 days. Once that 41st day rolled around I marked the blood as tossed and took it for myself. Who was to say if ethical consumption even existed? But I thought, considering the circumstances, I was pretty damn ethical.

"Do you... realize you glare at me? All the time?" Camron cleared his throat and shifted in the bed, not offering me an answer. His cheeks were red as if a fever were coming on. "Get some rest."

I left the bedroom and felt those sky blue eyes on the back of my neck. The fact I'd never sensed his nature till now gave me pause. So many factors and possibilities flooded my brain, the reality that I was not the only monster in town. When a wolf spotted a bear on the horizon did it feel fear— or comradery?

Just because I'd taken the day off didn't mean I couldn't work. I had plenty of emails and paperwork. Though I admitted I did spend a good amount of time emailing my patients who lived outside of town. Amongst their questions were update photos: wispy mustache hairs, breast buds over tee-shirts, and soft hips sometimes turning ample while others disappeared. I'd always been proud of my work, but these updates brought me a special joy. One I'd never expected anyone else in my life to understand. There was some joy in immortality, it seemed.

I lost track of time. When I looked up from my laptop,

Camron was standing in the bedroom doorway. "Excuse me?" I asked, exasperated. "Who said you could get out of bed?"

"Doc, come on, we're not at the hospital."

"Oh yes, we are," I practically laughed. "You showed up on my doorstep with a bullet wound. This is the closest thing to a hospital this town has." I rushed over to him and started leading him back toward the bed.

He obliged but as soon as he settled back onto the bed, brought up a good point. "I'm gonna have to relieve myself, you know. And eat. You don't have any food, do you?"

My fangs pressed against my bottom lip. "No... No, I don't have any food."

Camron raised a brow. "Can you leave the house? I feel like I've seen you in sunlight."

"Direct sunlight is the problem. If I stay away from windows in the clinic I'm fine. Summertime is the only real struggle." We were far enough north that it was dark most of the day three fourths of the year. Late June was my seasonal depression. "But no, I can't leave the house right now." I didn't even have to open the blinds to know the sun was hanging comfortably in the sky. I kissed my fangs, frustrated. "I might be able to call something in..." I said as if all my colleagues weren't busy at the clinic.

"I can get one of my guys to bring me something."

"Won't that raise suspicion? You hanging out at the doctor's cottage? People talk, Camron."

He snorted. "Yeah and a lot of that talk is bullshit anyway. My guys wanna be gossiping geese, so be it." I still didn't know how to feel about this. Reasoning would pop into my head, and before I could even rationalize that reason, another appeared in its place. A cellular mitosis of hypotheticals. Camron brought me back to reality. "Your call, Doc. Is food *really* that important?"

I could tell he was being sardonic. Which was earned.

"One moment," I told him before leaving to grab the landline.

He made a quick call to someone, asking them to drop off food at my stoop. "It can just be microwave shit. Wait, hold on." He lowered the phone and looked at me "Do you own a microwave?"

I nodded. I lived in a dollhouse. All the amenities I'd ever need yet they were all useless hunks of plastic. I didn't even keep them plugged in. Camron finished his call and looked at me expectantly. "What?" I huffed.

"You tell me. What do you usually do here? Hang upside down from the rafters?"

I rolled my eyes. "Clever, but no. I do all the things normal people do. Read, watch TV, when it's dark I go on hikes. Though now that I know there's wolves and hunters in the woods I should probably stop."

"I'd never hurt you Doc," he assured me. "I try not to hurt anyone."

"Try?" I inquired. Werewolves, I doubted, had the same bloodlust as us vampires. I kept myself well-fed enough that wounds didn't tempt me. Even so, it had taken many years of practice. Years of reminding myself of my role, of what I'd lose if I succumbed to my desire to drink from my patients. It was another reason I never drank from a living person. Cold turkey.

Camron ran his hands through his thick hair. "I'm a bit territorial. Mostly around the lumber yard. When the moon is full I'm drawn to it, I patrol it and if anyone gets close... Well..."

"You're really married to your job, huh?"

Camron cleared his throat. "You could uh, say that."

Two thoughts popped into my head. One: that whoever shot Camron likely knew about his 'territorial' nature. Which might help us figure out who the hell it was that was hunting him.

Two: Camron was a single man in his early forties with a good job and good social standing in town. I avoided gossip but I knew people had plenty to say about him being single at his age. I'd never heard about him having a girlfriend either. In this town, most people who started dating ended up together.

"I appreciate your passion. I'll admit I don't understand having such a love for lumber, but I do love my work."

"You think I like my job because of the wood?" As soon as he asked I realized how obtuse I was being. Of course it wasn't the fucking wood he liked. That would be like me enjoying the syringes at my job. Camron chuckled. "I guess you're not wrong. I love working in the woods."

"Conquering nature," I offered.

"No." He shook his head. "Working with it more like. Cut the dead limbs so the tree doesn't get top heavy and snap during a storm. And we're careful about what trees we cut. Even more, now that we've got this conservationist on the team. I like him, he kinda reminds me of you— passionate, you know?"

Did Camron think of me when I wasn't around? I tossed that question aside.

"I'm sure the trees appreciate it..." I offered. "I can admit now that in my era we weren't so interested in seeing the land for what it is. Only what it *could* be, after we marred it."

Camron quirked a thick brow. "How old are you, anyway?"

"Bit of a rude question, don't you think?"

"Shit, sorry." He shrugged. "But now the questions out there, I gotta know the answer. And if you don't tell me I'm just gonna guess." I licked my lips attempting to hide a smile, but Camron caught me and started rattling off dates. "Civil war— but the British one!" He spoke like a game show contestant.

"Refreshing you don't think I'm a Civil War vampire. Hate that stereotype."

"Am I right?"

"No. I'm not even British." I paused. "Wait, do I come off as British?"

"You come off as fancy," Camron elaborated then jumped to another theory. "Revolutionary war, the American one."

"What makes you think I'm from a wartime era? Is this the American education system at work?"

Camron snorted. "Shit, maybe. All I can think of is different wars."

"I'll give you one more guess. And a hint," I offered. "I lived through the American Civil War, but at that point, I was no longer human."

I watched the gears turn in his head. Then he blinked and his eyes went wide. "Oregon trail type shit?" I laughed, not expecting him to phrase it in that way. "I thought it was a pretty good guess..."

"It is," I assured him through my laughter. "It is, and you're right. I was born in Ohio and got swept up in the promise of untouched land and freedom. It was all a crock of shit but oh well."

Camron cocked his head. "You must have been pretty useful though. Being a doctor and all that."

"I was a midwife at the time. Not that it mattered. I still set a lot of bones and lanced a lot of wounds."

There was a knock at my front door. I left to go check and see who it was, peering carefully through the blinds on my front door. Someone had left a paper bag on my covered stoop. I held onto the doorknob, preparing myself for this little recon mission. My stoop was shaded but it was afternoon now, the sun at its boldest and brightest. I inhaled as if I needed to breathe, and held that breath in my chest. Turned the knob and my arm scraped against the doorframe as I snatched the paper bag. It was only a split second before I slammed the door shut. Of course, nothing happened, but any excursion outside during the day gave me anxiety.

Camron was standing in my kitchen. His lips pursed, obviously hiding a laugh. "You're welcome," I muttered. I set the paper bag on the counter and pulled out the spoils: hearty soups, popcorn, and jerky. "This sodium is going to kill you."

"Nah, I've got a good physician on speed dial." He smiled at me, and I felt foolish for thinking it wasn't the sort of smile shared between friends. That it was a grin for only special sorts of people.

"Do you actually have me on speed dial?"

My eyes started playing tricks on me, making me see the pink flush across Camron's cheeks as anything other than a symptom of his injury. "Well, yeah, considering how often I have to drag my guys into the office." He grabbed one of the soups and started tearing off the packaging. I watched him, admittedly fascinated with how streamlined food preparation had become. He literally just popped off the metal top and placed it in the microwave. That was it. Camron pressed some buttons and frowned.

"Oh," I chirped. I slid between him and the microwave, reaching back to plug the thing in. Once that was done, Camron reached past me and punched the buttons again. This time little beeps accompanied his touch. He pressed start and the microwave began to hum like the x-ray at work.

Then I felt Camron press his cheek against my neck. He was so warm, but everyone was so much warmer compared to me. I'm an ice pack— I told myself, that was all I was to him. Camron turn his head so his nose was pressed against my collar. "You always smell like elderflower..." He said.

I swallowed, my mouth suddenly dry. "I haven't the faintest idea why that would be."

"I don't care why," he rumbled. "I just know I like it."

The microwave screamed and I used it as a distraction to pull myself away from him. I caught myself on the kitchen island, gripping the mock marble. There were a million questions that would all stay neatly tucked away inside my head.

"Neatly" was being generous. The questions were overflowing like a single manilla folder stuffed with a ninety-six-year-old's case file.

It was made worse by an unfazed Camron, who grabbed his soup from the microwave and set it down across from me on the island. He riffled through kitchen drawers. One of my questions spilled out. "Why?" I stopped myself from adding any extra details.

"... I need a spoon."

I sighed, relieved that my question went right over his head. Opening my cutlery drawer, I handed him a spoon. He nodded and then went right to eating. I escaped to the living room and back into my work, hoping the charts would make me forget what had just happened.

NIGHT CAME and I opened up the curtains, letting in moon and starlight. The spot where Camron had smelled my supposed elderflower-skin still burned. Throughout the day I had touched the spot absentmindedly, fingers clawing at my dead flesh searching for the source of warmth. The mind is an expert at playing tricks on the body.

I went to Camron's room last, hoping to find him fast asleep. No such luck, he was sitting up in bed under the covers, his blue eyes locked onto me. I said nothing as I slid the curtains open. Afterwards, I saw his bloody jeans discarded on the floor. I picked them up and Camron cleared his throat.

"You can toss 'em."

I shook my head. "Really? You think I don't know how to get a little blood out?" He averted his gaze and I couldn't help but rib him a little more. "I'm just a doctor and a vampire. Obviously I've never had to clean up blood in my life. Hate the stuff actually." Camron hummed and turned his head even more, 'til all I could see was the back of his head.

This was the Camron I had expected to deal with all day. Distant and disapproving, like he'd rather be speaking to someone else. I folded his jeans and was ready to leave when my eyes happened to glance down at the bedsheets. I caught sight of a tent.

My upbringing got the best of me and I gasped, "Oh my."

"It's not you it's me—" Camron explained though he still wouldn't look at me. "I'm just uh... well you know how it is."

"I don't," I squeaked, then cleared my throat. "I mean, I do know, I understand anatomy." We were both quiet. "Could you at least look at me?"

"It's only going to get worse if I do."

"For fucks sake Camron it's a boner, not a rattler. And you said it has nothing to do with me."

His head snapped, looking in my direction. "I lied, okay?" It took me a second to process what he meant but he elaborated. "I've got a hard on because you're here, cause I think you're cute or some sappy shit."

I shook my head. "Sappy shit? Cute?" I stepped towards the bed, reaching to touch his forehead. "Have you spiked a fever?"

Camron grabbed my hand and pulled it to his lips, kissing my palm and then my wrist. "You smell so good..." he mumbled. He rubbed my hand along his cheek, like he was scenting me.

I crawled onto the bed. "I'm so confused," I admitted outright. "Do you... like me?"

It was Camron's turn to admit something. "I like pretty guys." He rolled my sleeve up my arm, kissing each new bit of pale flesh. "And you're wicked pretty, Doc."

"You always look so angry when we talk."

Camron winced. "Guess it's a little frustrating... and I'm trying to act all professional in front of the guys, you know."

I hesitated, not wanting to pry. "Do they know you're gay? Or, bi? Sorry, I shouldn't assume things…"

"Nah, I mean… I never settled on a label, so no, the guys don't know I like men. But they also don't know I like women, either."

I was glad there was vocabulary now for all sorts of attractions, words that encompassed myself and others. The solidarity that came from proudly proclaiming I was a gay man. But I also knew labels were imperfect, that there were some things that couldn't be put into words. I hoped Camron found solidarity somewhere.

"So you like me?" My question was clinical in tone. "For how long?"

"Yeah…" Camron leaned in, his lips almost touching mine. "You're always right about something, Doc. At first you freaked me out, I knew you weren't all human but didn't have a clue what you could be. Whenever there was an accident I'd wonder just what you are only to watch you be so… *good* to people." His voice dropped and I felt something within me crumble.

Since Camron's ill fated arrival my mind was made a storm, innumerable thoughts slipping through my fingers like wind. If I didn't catch them, if I couldn't pluck the right assertion from the air it would be the end of me… Those cold, calculated ideas prodding me like a fresh med student, eager and all too nervous. Then in my virgin bed those rushing thoughts floated up and away. His face was so close to mine— sun poking out through cloud cover… My eyes could not settle on one spot; his sky-blue eyes, square and stubbled jaw, his heavy brow, those lips still parted from his declaration.

Words fell from my lips like amber leaves off a branch. "You're very handsome."

"Careful, Doc," he warned. "You'll get me all excited."

I palmed his erection over the covers. Camron's pupils

dilated. "You're already excited." A puff of hot air hit my lips as he moaned. The bed creaked as he lifted his hips to grind against my palm. In reply, I began to press my thighs together, despite my better judgment. "We shouldn't," I thought aloud, the storm brewing once more.

"Why not?" Camron asked as his hand reached back to grab the nape of my neck.

I bit my lip so hard I expected my fangs to pierce my skin. "Because..."

"Because?" His gravelly voice mocked. His nose brushed against mine, leaving a trail of sunshine, as he had in the kitchen this afternoon.

"Fuck you, I can't think when you're humping my hand like this."

Camron pulled me to his lips. His tongue dove right into my mouth and I accepted it— wanting nothing but him. I pulled back the covers, then reached for his erection again, letting my hand run along the shaft. I felt something bulbous around the base and reached for it with my other hand while still stroking him. Camron pulled away from the kiss to curse. "Fuck Doc— you're going to make me finish."

"Can't you call me by my name while I'm touching you?"

He grinned. "This is basically a doctor's exam isn't it?" He pressed his forehead against mine. "At least 'til I get to shove my knot inside you." Then he grabbed my shoulder and pushed me down on the bed, our lips colliding once more. He ground his hips against my stomach, moaning into my mouth. "Levi." I took a handful of his hair and pulled his head back so his lips were free to speak. "Levi," he moaned again.

"Keep saying my name," I half sobbed. Loving his tongue pressing against his teeth for that L and hard E. The way he pulled on the V sound. Lee-vvye. Lee-vvye.

"I'll say whatever you want," he told me. I felt his hand reaching down for my pants. His fingers fumbled for a few moments before he got a hold of the button and slid it out of the hole. I helped him slide my pants off my legs. Then his hand returned to my crotch, wasting no time pressing his fingers inside me. "God, Levi, you're so wet already."

It was a surprise for me too. Between the vampirism, the testosterone, and not having had sex in a century I really didn't know how my body would react. Nor was I sure how Camron would react to... me. But he didn't hesitate for a second. He nipped at my neck while his fingers worked my cunt. His thumb ghosted along my thick clit and within moments my hips were lifted off the bed and I groaned like a banshee.

I tried to hide in Camron's neck but he reared his head back so he was looking right at me, a shit-eating grin on his face. "Already? That's so fucking hot..." He pulled back his fingers and pressed his length to my entrance. "You're so sexy, Levi. So fucking sexy. I wish I had more words for it." He sunk inside me ever so slowly and my head rolled into the mattress.

It was funny he complained about not having more words when I was incapable of articulating anything while he was inside me. Not that I needed to compel him as he started to pump his hips. He fell into a steady rhythm.

The whole time Camron's lips were pressed to my ear. "You feel so good baby, fuck— I should have *begged* for you. Begged to let me fuck you like this. Thank you for letting me fuck you, sweetness, my God—" He threw his head back, his teeth bared and jaw tight. Still inside me, he leaned back on his calves and then grabbed my hips, lifting them slightly. My shirt started to ride up along my chest. He pressed his hips into mine and I felt the resistance as his knot rubbed against me. "I don't want to hurt you, honey."

I reached up and cupped his cheek, appreciating his stubble. "The pain will pass," I breathed. "Give it to me." With that, he bucked his hips and his knot started to slip inside me. "More," I urged. With another thrust, he was comfortably inside me. I wrapped my calves around his body, keeping him as close to me as possible. Within a few moments, I felt his body shiver, his hips rutting against me desperately. He leaned down and I stroked his hair. "Give it to me," I breathed.

Warmth filled my cunt as Camron gasped and grunted. I continued stroking his blond hair as he came down. Only for him to growl a request. "Bite me." I thought I'd misheard when he spoke again with more force. "Feed from me."

"N-no!" I replied reflexively.

Camron pressed his forehead against mine, our noses pressed together. "Why not? Some hypocrite oath thing?"

"Hippocratic?"

He pushed his words past his teeth. "Yeah." Then he dove into my neck and started sucking at my skin. I expected him to bite me, give me a taste of the medicine he craved, but he didn't. He did manage to position his neck perfectly beside my lips. His heart was still racing from his orgasm. I could see the veins in his neck pulsing. I'd already given in once today— I wasn't sure if that gave me a pass or if it should make me all the more cautious.

I opened my mouth to speak. I felt my fangs already extended against my lips. I lunged like a rattlesnake, biting down on Camron's neck. He let out a sharp whimper, a sound I could never have imagined him making. Thick, warm blood pooled inside my mouth. Fresh. Flavorful. Warm. I shivered and felt Camron still deep inside me, his knot swollen.

He tasted like wintergreens and steak, rich yet fresh.

I was full within a matter of seconds.

I released his neck and then lapped at his wound, my saliva speeding up the coagulation process. I gave each puncture wound a little kiss before flopping back onto the mattress. My mouth was still tingling with the taste of evergreen mint. I watched Camron strain as he started to pull out. I relaxed and heard a pop followed by a feeling of emptiness.

Camron flopped beside me, wrapping an arm around me and pulling me close to his chest. "Did you cum?" he asked.

"In a way..." I told him. "I don't sleep but I feel like I could nap for ages. That's a side effect of the little death, no?"

"You asking me?" He raised his brows. "Shit— are you a virgin?"

I snort. "No, not in the slightest. But it has been a while." Longer than a while, but he didn't need to know that.

"Okay, good... I didn't think about how back in the day people waited."

"Oh, they didn't," I informed him. "I'm going to have to teach you a lot of history."

"I was never good in school," he admitted and I just hummed in reply.

I pulled away so I could slip out of my shirt, showing off the parallel scars from my surgery in the 50s. Snuggling up to him, indulging in his scent. He smelled like wood shavings and earth and I stifled a laugh as I realized he tasted just like he smelled. Then I became curious if his cum would somehow be minty as well. Camron didn't notice my attempt to hide my amusement. I noticed his eyelids were heavy. "Looks like you could use sleep as well."

He kissed his teeth. "Damn injury is taking more out of me than I thought. If I fall asleep... will you stay in bed with me?"

I nodded. "I don't have anywhere else to be."

CAMRON and I fell into a routine. We'd wake up— well, he would wake up. Have breakfast, again, Camron ate while I just watched him scarf down eggs. Then we'd go to work at our separate jobs. Not that it felt very separate when he'd come in with one of his guys. It was only a few days after our initial union that he appeared at the clinic.

"Come on Doc," the young man whined as I shined a penlight in his eyes. Camron mentioned something about him being a rookie to one of the nurses. It's rude to eavesdrop but I don't do it intentionally, heightened hearing and all.

"I had my helmet on," he whined, "A chunk of wood couldn't have done that much damage."

"Without your helmet it would have split your head."

His pupils shifted too Camron. "Shit, really?"

I cleared my throat, "Look forward please. And I'm not sure." I pretend Camron wasn't even in the room. "I was never great at physics."

Camron chuckled. I bit the inside of my lip and recalled all the days he would make that gruff sound in this room. I always assumed he was laughing at me, considered me paranoid. Knowing what I know now, having heard that sound in private, I think he found my comments endearing.

I finished up my examination. "No concussion from what I can tell. You're lucky." I wrote on my clipboard. "Just to be sure, no operating heavy machinery for the next few days."

"Doc, that's literally my job."

I looked to Camron for backup.

"Doctor's orders," he said with a shrug. "We can't afford to have another accident after today. You can do training. Maybe a refresher on safety protocols."

"I had my helmet! Man..."

Camron and I gave each other a look. "Could I speak to you in private, Mr. Coinin?"

"Shit," the rookie muttered. "Am I in trouble?"

Camron let out a huff of a laugh. "Nah, if anything I'm the one in the dog house." Then he shot me a cocky grin, obviously trying to get me to crack up. I remained stern.

We settled into my office. "Anyone acting—"

"Where'd you get those?" He pointed behind me.

It took me a moment to piece together his confusion but I looked back and saw my doctorate degrees. Of all the things in my office he could have fixated on "It's... complicated."

"Did you kill for those degrees?"

I scowl, just a touch offended by the accusation. "And if I did? My name is right there. Do you think I only kill men named Levi?"

Camron's gaze lowered and he mumbled to himself. "I don't think there are that many Levis..."

I opt to drop it and return to my question. "Has anyone at the site been shady?"

"Nah," he shook his head. "Wasn't any of them."

"Camron are you—"

"I'm sure, Levi. My guys wouldn't do this." I opened my mouth but he cut me off. "Even if they found out I was a werewolf."

"Don't say that so loud," I hissed.

"Why?" He cocked his head, not unlike a dog. "You think someone is listening in?"

"I love my staff but they can be nosey..." Hillary asked me why I'd been so smiley as of late. I didn't even realize I was doing it but I guess having Camron in my bed had an effect on me.

Despite my warning, my concern about us being the talk of our little town, I reached over my desk and took his hand. "I just want you to be safe."

"I will be." He placed one of his hairy, calloused hands over mine. "I got a good doctor to patch me up."

"Camron—"

He brought my hand to his lips and kissed my palm.

Damn him. Damn him and his romantic antics.

"I went to medical school."

Camron blinked, his thick brows knitted together.

"That's how I got the degrees on the wall. Medicine has

changed a lot in the past one hundred years. It would be negligent of me not to keep with the times."

"You're something else." He smiled. "Guess you wanna know about me now?"

I shook my head. "Haven't thought about it to be honest. Were you... born?"

"Turned. Got attacked while hiking by myself."

"At night?" Never mind the full moon. To those in the dark about these things, about the monsters that surround us, the appeal is there; a quiet trail illuminated by moonlight, the beautiful solitude the Romantics wrote poems about. The call of nature that dragged me out west. But Camron should have known better than to go hiking alone, let alone in the dead of night.

"I was a cocky teen. Fresh out of high school and had been fuckin' around in those woods all my life." He pulled his hand from mine and rubbed the back of his neck, embarrassed. I brought my own hand back to my desk. "Can't say I remember much—"

"That's good."

"Is it?"

"I wish I forgot when I was turned."

The room became silent, as dead as the empty as the plains where I was changed from man to monster. My fingers curled as I remembered that I was not alone when I was bitten. But by daylight, my companions were gone from this world.

Camron cleared his throat before standing up from his chair. "I should head back to the site. You know if you ever wanna talk—"

"Camron—"

"Levi." He practically sang my name. "We know what we are. Not many others do. Would be a waste to be cagey 'round each other." With that he left my office.

I turned around in my chair and looked up at my degrees. Class of '83. People wouldn't buy that for much longer.

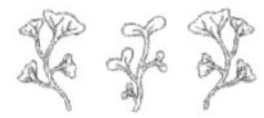

IT TOOK SOME TIME, a lot of hours sitting at my laptop on the google, but I found out where someone could get silver bullets. The answer was nowhere. But there was a forge an hour away in another tiny industrial town. That ended up being the smoking gun— pun intended. Not a lot of people smelt silver in the modern age.

The whole drive back to the cabin Camron went on and on. "Told you it wasn't one of my guys." The man at the forge was happy to tell us everything— especially after we mentioned where we were from. Someone else from our tiny town had been driving up to the forge for one, strange purpose. Smelting silver bullets.

"Okay," I huffed, "And? What do you want me to say?"

"That I was right." Camron exasperated. I found it sort of charming that he wanted me to praise him so bad.

I reached over and touched his knee. "You were right. None of your guys would want to hurt you. You're a good boss after all."

A confident grin spread across his face as he drove, myself glad that he was right in the end. Though he smiled his words were grim, as grey as the sky above. "He'll come back next full moon. He got pretty damn close to ending me, second time the charm you know."

The clouds taunted us with rain, a constant teasing like a child sticking out their tongue. I grimaced. "If you're right that means he might *actually* kill you this attempt. No one wants that. Least of all me." A light drizzle was warranted for our conversation, but it never came.

Camron nodded. "But this time there will be two of us. This guy— what's his name again?"

"Jack Mason. He comes into the clinic fairly often, he had gout a few years ago—"

"Wait, people can still catch gout?"

I rolled my eyes. "Cam, you can't *catch* gout."

"Right, right," he continued to nod. "But that's a good thing isn't it?" I furrowed my brows not sure what he's getting at. "I mean, if you know him better than me, and he doesn't suspect you're not a human, then he won't expect you next full moon."

He had a point— but I still didn't like this plan. One lucky shot to Camron's heart or head and it would be over. The same could be said for myself. Silver is effective against all manner of supernatural beings, but I'm not the intended target. Not to mention I hadn't killed anyone in a century. I wasn't sure if Camron had ever killed.

My angst distracted me and I didn't notice Camron pulling off to the side of the road. The concrete structure had blacked out windows and I innocently assumed we were just stopping for fuel. Except there weren't any fuel pumps.

"Camron..." I said his name incredulously, squinting at the buildings darkened windows.

He leaned over and pointed at a small, unlit neon sign near the door: *Petey's Pleasures*.

"Absolutely not."

"What?" Camron shrugged before hopping out of the car.

I had no choice but to follow, though in hindsight I could have just waited in the car. But my curiosity got the better of me. Even with the cloud cover I hid beneath the lumber company hoodie of Cam's I'd taken as my own. "Why?"

"Because we fuck?" He said too loud for my own comfort as he opened the door.

There was a series of bells that made a charming jingling sound as we entered. It was a stark contrast to the rest of the store, the walls painted an obnoxious pink while the floors were drab linoleum you would find in any roadside convenience store. The lights were a harsh white like that of an operating room. Everything smelled of plastic.

I followed Camron, keeping my eyes very intentionally on his back. He hummed a laugh and picked something off the wall: a set of white lacy lingerie. "What do you think?"

I made a face like he was handing me a plate of food and expecting me to gobble it up. "I am never wearing that."

"I meant for me."

My brain started to melt. The image of Camron in all his glory, the delicate lace alongside his thick hairy chest and his cock straining against the near translucent fabric... Camron, thankfully, started laughing and put the underwear aside. If he had pushed it, I'm not sure I would have been able to lie.

No longer focused on my lover I started to take in the rest of the store. Mannequins wearing what I suppose could be called clothes, phalluses of ridiculous sizes and colors, condoms with fruit plastered across them, plenty of things I did not recognize, and a wall of DVDs. "Do... you shop here often?"

"I uh..." Camron rubbed the back of his neck. "Like supporting local business? Look, the porn here is just better."

"Better than what? Your imagination?"

He took my hand and started leading me around the store, bringing me to a display of bottles. There were an array of product names, some water based, others silicone, but they were all lubricants of some sort. I picked up one and examined it. "Do you want to use condoms?"

He rubbed the back of his neck. "Ah..."

I glanced up at him. "Don't tell me that question has you flustered. Standing in here of all places."

"It's just we haven't been using them so far. Kind of a weird question."

I shook my head. "You can't use a silicone based lube with silicone, it'll cause it to deteriorate. But if we're not using protection..."

Camron gingerly took the bottle from my hand and put it back. "We might want toys or something."

I choked on nothing. "Wh-why would we need that?"

"Hey, hey," he rubbed my back. "We don't *need* them, I just thought they might be fun."

"I am not," I pointed vaguely toward the phallic toys I'd seen before, refusing to actually look at them. "Putting those inside me."

Camron bent down. "It's not all about you." He kissed my cheek, then whispered in my ear. "You don't want to try topping me?"

Though I'd never stepped foot in a sex shop I was well aware of the options. They'd been introduced to me by my queer counterparts, though not intimately. I was always hesitant to sleep with humans. Still am. But that didn't stop the leather daddy with a hanky out his back pocket from courting me— nor the stone butch offering me her strap. Of course I declined them both, but it was flattering all the same.

"Why don't we start with lube," I told him.

We both examine the bottles, arguing the pros and cons of each one. It occurred to me this was rather domestic, finding something we could both enjoy. If only we weren't standing in a damn sex shop. Still, we settled on a lube specifically for anal. A large bottle, which I thought was a bit presumptuous.

"I'm sure I could have just borrowed some from work," I mentioned to Camron as he studied the walls of the store.

Instead of responding to my statement, he grabbed an object off the wall and showed it to me. "What about this?" He shows me a package with what looks like a thick rubber band.

It took me a moment to connect what it was he was holding. "Oh God," I covered my cheeks.

Camron snorted and I became convinced he was trying to

make me spiral. "Why do I feel like if you had any blood you'd be tomato red right now?"

I frowned. "If I had any blood I think I would have passed out by now."

"Is this really that much? I don't get how a doctor can be freaked out by sex."

"I'm not—" I start, much too loud. I noticed the store's attendant looking over at us. "I'm not freaked out by sex," I said softly. "Kinky sex, I'll admit, is a bit outside my knowledge."

Camron nods. "We could fix that."

"You would like that, wouldn't you?"

"We've already done a bit of blood play."

I snatch the cock ring out of his hand. "We're getting the lube and leaving."

As I placed the toy back on the wall, I felt the coarse hairs of Camron's beard brush my cheek before he kissed me there. "You know I'm teasing, right?"

I pursed my lips. "I wish you wouldn't."

"But it's fun. You're always so strait-laced."

He took my hand again and we walked to the register, purchasing the lube without a single word. Back in the car, the bottle sat in my lap.

"Am I really that much of a stick in the mud?"

"Nah," he shook his head. "You're just real proper." One hand left the wheel and he reached down to touch my thigh. "I'm sorry if that was... too much."

"It was unexpected," I admitted. "I didn't realize you wanted to... experiment."

"I don't see why not," he shrugged. "I meant it, you can top me if you wanna. I like both." His eyes were focused on the road, almost avoidant like in the bedroom our first night together.

It's too easy to tease him back after that ordeal. "And when you said the porn there is better?"

"Ah," he hummed, his jaw went a bit sideways. "I just know what I like and I'd rather have a whole hour's worth instead of a few minutes, ya feel me?" He shot me a goofy grin. "Well— I guess not."

"The last time I saw an adult film it was in the theater."

Camron laughed. "The good old days."

It's dark by the time we got home, which gave us the opportunity to hold hands and casually walk back to the cabin. There was something about Camron's eyes in the moonlight that made me sad I would never see them under the full moon. He must have noticed me admiring him, because once we're on the deck he pulled me to his body and kissed me hard. He held the back of my head, pushed my head against his lips.

In his arms I feel a part of him. The only person I knew who I could be completely honest with. My body and its flaws are sanguine to him. He didn't make me feel alive, but he made me feel okay about being dead.

I pulled away from his lips just enough to breathe against them. "We should get inside." I grabbed the collar of his shirt and led him to the door. He didn't fight, following me obediently. As soon as we were past the door he started to kick off his boots. I did the same. With each step another article of clothing dropped to the ground, abandoned.

By the time we reached the bedroom, we were both nude. "Sit on the edge of the bed," Camron's voice rumbled in my ear. I did as he said, finding comfort in following his will. Camron fell to his knees in front of me, looking up at me with reverence. I ran my fingers through his beard.

"There are so many things I want to do with you Levi..." He kissed my knee, then pulled my legs apart. "Sexually, spiritually, emotionally," he accented each word with a kiss along my inner thigh.

Living as long as I had I thought soulmates were bullshit. I would have to revisit such an assertion.

Camron's lips found my cock, protruding out from my labia. He sucked at it, the bottom of his tongue caressing it, holding it up. I moaned and my hand found his hair, stroked it, praised him without words. He buried his face between my thighs, tongue running along my cunt and thick clit. He moaned and I felt the vibrations all up my body.

When he pulled his face away, his beard had droplets of slick that shone like his eyes. "Sit on my face. Please, Levi."

As if he needed to beg.

He got up on the bed and laid down. I straddled his face, looking down to catch a glimpse of him grinning. I lowered myself, sitting comfortably on his chin and nose. His tongue filled me and my head fell back as I cried out. "Camron—" I ran my fingers through his hair and tugged at it. His tongue somehow buried itself deeper inside me. I could no longer form words, just whimpers and moans.

I moved my hips, my cock grinding against his nose. I reached down, my fingers spreading my folds so more of my cock could touch his face. Camron's eyes were closed, I knew in pleasure, but it felt like an insult.

"Look at me," I shouted, unable to control my voice.

His blue eyes opened wide. I wanted to tell him to watch me as I came but my shallow breaths told him all he needed to know. I practically sobbed as I finished on his tongue, the two of us lost in each other's eyes.

Camron grabbed my hips and helped me off his face, laying me on my side. He wrapped his arms around me, pressing his face against my chest. His beard was even more soaked then. The grin from before remained. "You taste so good, darlin'. Even better than you smell..." He whispered to me.

It was impossible to look away from his face, his pure bliss. But my hand reached down to touch his cock, so hard it touched his round stomach. I stroked him and he hummed in approval. I brought my lips to his ear. "Why don't you shove your cock down my throat?" Camron grunted. "Do you want to fuck my throat?"

"Absolutely..." he moaned.

I let go of his girth and shifted my body so my head hung off the side of the bed. Camron slid off the bed, standing in front of me as he stroked his cock. He chuckled, "Didn't realize what a freak you could be Levi..." He ran the head of his cock along my lips. "I'm such a lucky bastard."

I took his cock in my mouth and Camron pushed his hips. I felt him slide to the back of my mouth and down my throat. It wasn't as if I needed to breathe. He held his position, letting his girth rest inside my throat, his balls against my forehead. I couldn't see his face, but I could hear his moans, feel his cock twitch against my tongue. Camron began to pull out and I made sure my lips were wrapped around him, like a ribbon wrapped around the present.

The head of his cock left my mouth with a pop. "Damn, sweetheart." He wrapped his hand around my throat. "I don't know if I'll be able to contain myself..."

I responded by opening my mouth wide, letting my tongue rest against my chin. Camron smacked his cock against my tongue before sliding it inside my mouth again. Holding onto my throat as leverage he started to buck his hips. The deeper the thrust the harder he gripped my neck. There was a special bliss in knowing I was the only person who could give him this. Who he could fuck without fear of destroying completely.

Camron spoke between gritted teeth. "Fuck— oh fuck me, darlin'."

Lewd, wet sounds filled the room, spit rolling down my cheeks. I felt every inch of his fingertips dig into my throat. Were I capable of bruising I would have looked a mess. Not that I didn't look ravished, covered in spit, eyes wide and wet.

His knot struggled to pass my lips, and I opened my mouth wider. Camron grabbed his knot with his free hand

and helped push it inside my mouth, my lips wrapping around what couldn't fit. I barely managed a hum, my throat much too full with him. I could hear Camron struggled to catch his breath, but he released my neck—stroking it with his fingers. "Beautiful... You're beautiful..." He breathed. I wondered if he could feel his touch the way I felt him bulge inside my throat.

He pulled back, just enough for his knot to exit my mouth. He placed his hands on either side of my torso and started moving his hips again. He fucked my throat like the hole it was— his to claim, his to use as he pleased.

"Levi— shit, I'm close."

I reached back and grabbed his ass, encouraging him to fuck me faster. Cameron choked on a broken moan just before he filled my throat, and I lamented that he was too deep inside me for me to taste it. But as he pulled out of my throat I refused to let him go, my tongue pressing against his length. Desperately lapping at the tip trying to get a taste. There was a faint, salty flavor on the tip of my tongue when he pulled himself from my lips and I whimpered.

Camron stroked my cheek. His face was flushed and his shoulders heaved as he caught his breath. "Are you," he cleared his throat. "You okay?"

I licked my lips though they were already soaked with spit. "Finish in my mouth next time."

"Not on your face?" He chuckled.

I grimaced. "That seems messy," I told him. "And I want to taste you..."

"After that? Baby, I'll do whatever you want next time."

He crawled back onto the bed and pulled me into his arms, kissing my throat. I ran my fingers through his beard, still wet with my slick. "Was I too rough?" He asked, cheek pressed against my collar.

"Not at all."

"Are you sure?"

"Damn sure," I informed him.

We fell back onto the pillows, looking at each other, stroking each other. I loved his hairy chest and thighs, loved reaching back to grab his ass and watch him smile as my nails dug into his flesh. He always touched my cheeks, brushed my hair aside, ran his thumb along my top-scars. The mattress was still firm having only been used a handful of times in a decade. I wondered how long it would take to become worn, to bend beneath us and hold our shapes.

Despite our bliss, I couldn't hide any longer.

"I'm scared," I whispered.

"What are you scared of, baby?" He pushed some hair behind my ear.

"Of losing you... Of seeing you get hurt again."

My fingers find the spot were his stitches once laid. There was no scar, no proof, a mythological sort of wound. It's mean to admit, but I expected him to shrug off my concerns. To act all tough and macho about it— act like he's invincible when we both know he's not.

Instead, he kissed the crown of my head. "I don't want either of us getting hurt," he told me. "Hell, that bullet hurt like a bitch so I'd rather not go through that again. But of course, I'd rather get hurt than you."

"Don't say that."

He shrugged. "Already did... and it's how I feel." He cupped my face in his big, calloused hands. "I'm going to kill that motherfucker."

"Don't—"

"Levi, we don't have much of a choice." His thick brows furrowed. "Either we end this now or it follows us. I'd rather spend the rest of my days in peace with you than looking over my shoulder afraid of some guy with goddamn gout."

I tried to shake my head but his hands held me in place. "I don't like hurting people."

"Course not, you're a healer, it's not in your nature to hurt. But just this once you've gotta. For us."

I pursed my lips. "For us..."

THE FULL MOON arrived as it did every month: with little fanfare.

I stood on a tree branch looking down at the main logging site. Cam was below, pacing the perimeter. He was much more wolfish than he'd been when he arrived at my doorstep a month ago. His entire body was covered in a thick hide and even from up high, I could see his eyes glowing in the night. I could see the moonlight reflecting off his teeth as well, his maw always hanging open. If I didn't know that it was Camron in that big furry body, I'd be terrified.

It was starting to get boring standing about when I heard a branch snap in the opposite direction of Cam's pacing. I turned, grabbing onto a branch above to steady myself. Through the brush it was hard to see where the sound came from... possibly it was just some harmless creature. Or it wasn't and my carelessness would get Camron killed. There was another distinct snap and I decided that was enough for me to go investigate.

I hopped from the branches, practically floating. I couldn't explain it but vampires were just lighter, like the rules of gravity only half applied to us. It wasn't an ability I thought about or used often. But it was indispensable as I jumped from branches and trees to reach the sound below. Finally, I saw him. Jack, stalking through the woods, his face covered in cloth and his balding head covered in a hat. But I knew it was him because he had a rifle and no safety vest on. Exactly like last time.

What happened to you? I wondered, my empathy taking over. I shook my head, forced myself to block out the little things I'd learned about Jack after being his primary doctor for the past three years. He was divorced, he made a mean veal stew, he got thrown from an ATV as a kid and had the scar to prove it.

Right now, he was just a threat, like a cancerous lump.

I touched down on the forest floor, the leaves beneath my feet not even cracking under my weight. Attacking from behind felt cheap— but I knew Jack gave Camron no such courtesies.

I pounced, struggling to get at his neck with his cowl in the way, but eventually, my fangs pierced his neck. He didn't struggle. No one ever did. Once the bite was initiated, victims tended to fall into a relaxed state— or perhaps shock. It didn't matter. What mattered was I had him and he tasted like fresh bread. Beyond taste, his blood was warm and comforting, like how I remembered fresh bread. Melting on my tongue, filling me body and soul.

I couldn't possibly drain him dry so I did the merciful thing and snapped his neck. Then I placed him on the ground, not sure what to do next.

When I licked my fangs I could still taste him. His after-taste was more akin to hops than wheat, like beer. He'd told me he'd cut alcohol out of his diet. I didn't have it in me to be annoyed at him for lying. I was still standing over his body when Camron wandered over. He was much taller in his wolf form, almost seven feet. He picked up Jack's body with ease and wandered deep into the woods. Ignorance was bliss and it was for the best I didn't know what happened to Jack's body. Though I knew exactly what happened to a body left out to the elements.

I wandered back to the job site and got into Camron's truck. He'd left the keys in the ignition so I could drive myself home before the sun came up. Said he'd get a ride home from one of his coworkers. The drive was unmemorable and I was in a haze the whole way back. I got into my cabin and flopped onto the bed, my face flat against Cam's pillow. It smelled of him; pine like the woods I'd fled, rich earth, a hint of his vanilla shampoo. I wrapped my arms around it and pulled it closer to my face. *For us...*

I WAS LEAVING the kitchen holding a blood bag when Camron stopped me. "Where are you taking that?"

I hesitated. "Um... the bathroom..." I didn't want him to watch me feed. I could ask him to leave the kitchen but that felt rude. I was the one being an inconvenience.

Though Camron's expression said otherwise. "Levi, I am not grossed out by your drinking habits. It's just blood."

Despite my fear that his stomach would say different once he saw me feed, I ended up staying. I attached a short Y-tube to the bag and drank from it like a smoothie. The whole time I just thought about how Camron tasted so much better than this bagged blood.

Camron didn't watch me eat, which I appreciated. Instead, he was reading a book about medical practices in the 1800s. "Did you guys really use maggots?"

"Cam, I'm eating." I reminded him. "But yes. It was a very effective way to get rid of rotted flesh. Of course, we would never do something like that now. But back then we couldn't sterilize medical instruments like we do now. Especially field medicine."

Camron shuddered and closed the book. "You've got a gnarly job, Levi."

I smiled, very intentionally showing off my fangs. "Thanks." I took a long pull from the blood bag. Camron got up and walked over to me, wrapping his arms around my waist while I still had the tube in my mouth. The corners of his lips were downturned slightly. I thought he was about to ask me to go hide away in the bathroom to finish up my meal.

Instead, he asked, "Why don't you just feed off me?"

I blinked. "Well... I didn't think you'd want to?"

"Why wouldn't I want to?"

I set my bag of blood on the counter, careful to lay the tube so none of the blood spilled out. "Feeding off someone feels so barbaric."

"But that's about you. Not about me." His head tilted to the side. "It felt kinda nice when you drank from me before. And you don't need all that much do you?"

"I've lived off one pint a week for a century. I'm not sure if I took more or less when I fed from you. Probably less..."

"Yeah but one pint isn't that much. There's gotta be like, a hundred pints of blood in my body."

"You're wrong. Ten times over." Camron looked a bit offended so I explained further. "You, and everyone else, have ten pints of blood in their body. You can't possibly give me a pint of your blood every week, it's not sustainable."

He nodded his head. "Okay... What about once a month? Can we try that? I want to be able to give you something."

"You give me plenty."

"Then I want to give you more."

I knew I wasn't going to be able to talk him down from this. He wanted me to feed from him— and I was grateful. But it just felt so antithetical to the work I do. "I'm willing to try. But you have to let me say no if I just... can't." I shook my head. "I have to get used to having a person be my source of life instead of a bag." Just as I needed time to adjust when it was the opposite, before blood could be preserved and there was no choice to be had. Feed from the living or from the newly dead, the latter felt just a ghoulish.

"Did you not like feeding from me last time?" He looked a little hurt. I wished I could understand why he wanted this so bad— I blamed all those vampire books.

"Cam, that entire experience was ethereal, but you were also inside me. The context matters."

He nodded some more. "Right, gotcha. We could always only feed when we're fuck—" I smacked him on the chest and he laughed. "Okay, so not that. But we'll try and see." He lowered his head to press his forehead against mine. It was his favorite way to show affection, I'd realized. I loved it too. It somehow felt more intimate than kissing. "We can try things, and if they don't work that's okay."

His eyes were closed but I couldn't help but just stare at him. He surprised me every day. Sometimes those surprises were rude awakenings and sometimes they were welcome surprises. Like right now. After centuries there was finally someone in my life who kept me on my toes, to kept things interesting.

I wrapped my arms around his neck and kissed him. Then I pulled myself up by his neck, wrapping my legs around his thick waist. Camron chuckled into the kiss as he helped me up, taking hold of my thighs and lifting me onto the kitchen counter. His sharp canines caught my bottom lip and I whimpered before I was able to catch his lips again. My fangs pulled at his lips as well, but mine tore just a bit of his skin. I sucked on his bleeding lip, my mouth filling with his fresh, almost minty taste. Camron groaned, not pulling away as I sucked at his wound.

Finally, I lapped at the little cut and it closed immediately. I said to Camron, "Bedroom."

"We should put this away first, right?" He lifted up the blood bag.

If I'd had the ability to blush I would have. "Right." I stored the bag back in the fridge, hoping to remember it after we'd finished pawing and fucking each other. Though after our conversation, maybe Camron would fill me in more ways than one.

As we walked to the bedroom I started stripping, leaving my shirt and pants on the living room floor. Camron hummed behind me. "I don't know why, but I love seeing you in those boxers." He grabbed his groin, tugging at his cock over his jeans as he walked.

As soon as we were in the bedroom he pushed me onto the bed and I landed on my chest. He got on top of me, grinding his jeans against my ass while he pinned me down, both of us completely flat against the mattress. Despite his manhandling he kissed my ear softly. Before growling, "I have an idea... are you cool to do anal tonight?"

"I'd love that," I breathed. He started kissing my neck. "Take your jeans off already."

Camron fell back on his calves and I heard him fiddling with his belt. Still on my stomach, I reached for the bedside table and grabbed our recently purchased lube. Upon reflection I was grateful for the visit to *Petey's Pleasures*. Camron had no shame, no hesitation in being indecent and intimate with me. My bygone heart needed some time to adjust but I wanted— needed, to give him everything he desired. Somewhere in the catacomb of my soul my lust for him only grew, affection its bedmate.

Holding onto the bottle, Camron pulled down my boxers before flipping me over so I was on my back. He was completely naked and his cock stood at attention. He leaned down with a smirk across his lips. "Thanks, sweetness" he kissed my cheek before taking the lube from my hands. I watched him dab some lube on his fingers and rub them together. Then he reached down between my cheeks and started massaging my hole.

"I want you to touch yourself." He didn't have to tell me twice as I reached down and stroked my cunt and cock. My breathing became heavy as both my holes received attention. Camron slipped a finger inside my ass, then another. We moved our fingers in tandem— filling and emptying me. "That's it," Cam's voice rumbled. "That's what I want to see."

I sighed, my eyes on Camron's hips, admiring the trail of hair down his stomach. He was plenty hairy but his happy trail was especially impressive. Distracted, I hardly noticed he'd stopped fingering my ass, grabbing his cock to slip inside me. It was a welcome feeling and I just sighed with content. Then he released my wrist to instead stroke my small cock. He took it between his fingers, caressing it, stroking it. Then he started bucking his hips, grunting through his tight jaw.

"Camron, fuck—" I choked out as my fingers grabbed at the sheets.

"You like that don't you, honey?"

"Y-yes," I stammered.

"Baby, you fucking love it, don't you?"

I shouted, "Yes!"

As if to reward me Camron's thumb plunged inside me, pressing up and against my g-spot. It was enough to make me cum, the bedroom filling with a chorus of my screams and the sound of ripping sheets. Camron let up on my small cock, but his thumb and cock were still deep inside me as I rode out my orgasm.

As I laid in bed, glassy-eyed and slack-jawed, Camron chuckled. "We're going to need new sheets."

"Let's ruin these more first..." Always so aware of my needs, Camron leaned down and kissed me. He moved his hips again. Slower this time, really letting me appreciate the power behind his thrusts.

He only released my lips to praise me. "Your body is so perfect," he muttered. "I love fucking your holes," he shoved his tongue down my throat before finishing his thought. "And jerking you off." Again his lips were on mine and all I could do was moan in appreciation. He was so good to me. I just wish I'd seen it sooner.

"I should have told you my feelings long ago," Camron told me just before he pushed his knot inside me. Immediately after he began gasping and groaning, like he always did when he came.

Then he collapsed on top of me and I had to laugh. I pointed out the obvious. "You're crushing me." He hummed in reply. I started playing with his hair, letting him fall into a sense of security before I took a handful and yanked his head back.

Camron hissed, his sharp sound became a deep chuckle. "Fine," he kept laughing to himself as he rolled us both over onto our sides. He couldn't seem to stop laughing. "Better?"

How could I say no to that smile? "So much better. Better with you here." I leaned in and could tell from the way Camron closed his eyes he was expecting a kiss. But I went right for his neck— surprising him when the tips of my fangs scraped his neck.

He let out a whine, not unlike a dog's. So I bit down, my fangs piercing his external carotid artery. Camron held me tight, quivering as I drank from him. All while his knot kept me stretched open. I sucked at his neck, not even needing to, his artery did all the work for me. But I wanted to leave an extra reminder of this moment. Still sucking at his sensitive skin, my tongue ran along the wounds I'd inflicted. Once I was sure they were closed I released his neck.

The ghosts of my fangs were framed perfectly by an early bruise, the same vibrant red as his blood. Camron chuckled. "Just what the doctor ordered."

Jack Mason was found dead, floating face down in the river a few days after the full moon.

The coroner— myself, seeing as the only morgue in town was in my clinic, labeled it an accident. Either he slipped and fell or maybe his heart gave out and he rolled into the river. The how didn't seem to really matter much. No one asked too many questions of me.

His daughter came in from out of town to identify him. "I'm surprised I can see him," she told me. "I thought he might have offed himself."

Apparently he'd been acting strange. Claimed there was

something in the woods. Said he *knew* there was something out there. "Aliens, Bigfoot, hell knows what. He wouldn't tell me and to be honest doctor..." I looked at the girl who I prescribed birth control before she went off to college in Seattle. "I don't think I would have listened either way."

Everyone in town came to the funeral. There wasn't much else to do that Saturday. Not to mention everyone knew Jack. Just as everyone knew Meryl the waitress at the one diner in town or Mr. Green the high school's chemistry teacher and basketball coach. Just as everyone knew me, knew Camron. But didn't know us.

The funeral was a closed casket, featuring a big portrait of Jack from a few years back. There was a light in his eyes I hadn't seen in a while. Then again what sort of glimmer could I have found last I saw him, stalking my lover in the woods, wishing him dead. I avoided Camron during the funeral but caught his eye when he stepped up to the casket to pay his respects.

Almost everyone came up to me, shook my hand. "Thanks Doc." How ignorant.

I didn't follow the procession of cars to the cemetery. There was too much sunlight that day. It was only when I pulled up to my cabin I realized Camron's truck had been following me. He got out first, holding one of his old flannels. I held it over my head like I was avoiding rain and we made our way back into my cabin.

I laid on the couch in my suit wishing I had the ability to sleep. I missed the parts of humanity no one expects; resting, enjoying a sunny day, smelling blood and feeling revulsion instead of hunger...

As if he could read my mind, Camron came over, kneeled next to the couch. He looked nice in his black suit and navy tie. It felt wrong to be smitten with him in funeral attire. But as he slipped off his suit jacket and rolled up his sleeve, I remembered Camron doesn't mind me being a monster.

He offered me his wrist. I supposed it was a bit like drinking a beer or having a shot... I held onto his wrist, kissing his veins before sinking my teeth into them. Blood filled my mouth faster than I could drink, his artery pushing more and more into my mouth. It really was like taking a shot. I pulled my teeth back and pressed my tongue against his wrist, stopping the bleeding.

I swallowed the last remnants of blood in my mouth. Then examined his wrist, making sure the wound was completely closed. Two perfect circles marred his wrist, vibrant red against his icy blue veins. Still holding his wrist my other hand reached for him, pressing two fingers against the side of his neck.

"Levi I'm fine, it couldn't have even been that much."

I ignored him. As wonderful as Camron was I wished he would let me be my paranoid self every once in a while. It's only kept me alive for the past two hundred years.

"One-fifty," I say as if there's a nurse in the room to write down my report. "Not great, Camron."

"Isn't a big number good? Means I've got a strong heart, right?"

I sigh, not sure I have it in me to explain it all to him.

He pulled his wrist away then placed his hand over mine. "Dear, why you gotta be so melancholy?" My mouth was still warm from his blood. "No one is going to hurt us anymore."

"Except you."

Camron blinked. Shook his head a little like I'd just asked him a question he couldn't answer. "Camron one day you will die. You'll die and I'll be all alone again. It's not anyone's fault. It's just a fact of life."

He's my lifeline in the sense that the day he does die, I know I'll never truly feel alive again.

"What do you want me to say?" He frowned. "That I'm okay with hurting you?" I glanced down and he grabbed my chin, turned my head forward to face him again. "Cause if the options are leaving you now— running into you at the clinic and dreaming about you at night, or staying and leaving you when I'm an old geezer, I'm holding onto you Levi. Selfish as that is."

Camron's hand slipped from my chin and I returned to looking at anything other than him. I settled on my hands, pale and lifeless.

He kissed his teeth. "Aight, I get it..." He stood up and I sat up in response, afraid he might stumble from the blood loss. But he got up no problem and walked to the kitchen, opening the fridge to get himself a beer. I watched him from behind the couch as he knocked the beer back.

Camron Coinin how I wished the world could know you the way I do. Experience your soft touch and taste your sweetness. To know that you could be so terrible; a bad boss, a monstrous werewolf, just another man with a piss-poor attitude. If only it was me that would someday die and leave a hollow spot where I once stood. That's my selfish desire: to be missed. To have him fear missing me.

"I think I'm in love with you."

Camron sputtered, foam dripping from his lips. He looked at me with wide eyes as he wiped the dribbling beer from his lips and chin. There was a heavy swallow. "Really?"

"You make me feel... Not alive. But not dead— even though that's what I am. Somehow when I'm with you I never forget that I'm far gone from humanity... yet I look at you and it feels like my heart is racing."

Camron pursed his lips then cleared his throat, setting the beer down on the counter. "I... I uh..." He placed both hands on the counter and leaned against it, like it was the only thing keeping him standing.

"Perhaps you shouldn't have drank right after having your blood drawn." I couldn't resist commenting.

"Shit, Levi, I'm trying to think here. You know I'm not so poetic."

I stood up on the couch and hopped over the back to join him in the kitchen. He raised his finger. "Hey, hold on now, give me a second—"

"What?" I snorted.

"I don't wanna kiss you till I've made my confession. Cause I love you too—" I started to reach for his face. "Wait, wait! I gotta say something memorable."

Laughter bubbled up from my gut. In an instant I forgot about the funeral, about how I'd taken a father and a friend from this world, ignored my broken oath... I did it all for Camron. I did it all for us. As I watched him, flustered and red faced, I realized if I focused on all the ills I'd lose precious time with him. I can't change my past. At least in the present, I had him. Our future was hard-fought.

He closed his eyes and took a deep breath. "Levi you're smart and sexy and more than I probably deserve. I know you'll tell me I'm wrong, that you're the one less deserving, but I think for all your brains you got a screw loose somewhere. You..." His voice wavered. "*I've* been alone for so long. You for much longer and I can't imagine it. But maybe we can empathize— move past that solitude. I'm one lucky dog of a man. And I love you. I love you so damn much."

Camron claimed to be far from a poet but I failed to recall anything that matched his words. "Can I kiss you now?"

He opened up his arms. "Please do, darlin'."

I didn't like being sappy, but I leapt into his arms and kissed him so hard our teeth knocked together. Camron just chuckled, his hands firm on my ass holding me up off the floor.

My lips left his but I brushed my nose against his. "I'm sorry... for being so..."

"Mopey?" He offered. "I'm used to it. I think. Guess when you've lived a long time, people tend to get a bit dreary."

"I want you to stay," I assured him. "I just wish you could stay forever. That's *me* being selfish."

"I don't think so. I think even humans wish their loved ones could live forever. Most of us don't though." He kissed the corner of my mouth. "Then I'm going to make you as happy as I can for as long as I live..." He whispered and his forehead found mine. "So then it'll hurt even worse when I pass."

I chuckled. "Bastard."

WE FOUND ourselves back at *Petey's Pleasures*— by my request. I pushed the door open while Camron followed. His head hung low between his shoulders. "You're walking fast."

That I may have been. Though I'd been skittish before I had a good recollection of where everything was kept in the store; the wall of cheap lingerie, the flavor condom display, the rack of DVDs, I ignored all of them. We make it to the leather section and I grabbed a harness off the wall.

Camron snorts. "You sure you want that one? Take a breath, dear." I opened my mouth for a rebuttal. "I know you don't need to breathe. Cheeky."

"Not a fan of the leather?" I offered.

"Just want to make sure it's what you want. Especially with that price tag."

I examined the straps, ran my thumb over the silver O ring. Still fully dressed I stepped through the straps. Cam jumped then looked around the store as if it weren't a ghost town of pleasure. I finished tightening the straps around my legs and kept running my palms along the leather, appreciating its softness.

Cam swallowed, blue eyes as wide as the ring that rested flush against my crotch. His cheeks were pinker then they had been when we walked inside.

"This will work." As I pulled the bar back on the buckle, I told Cam, "You can pick out the rest."

He cleared his throat. "You want me to pick your dick?"

"Sure." I shrugged. "It's for you anyhow. I'm plenty happy with two inches but I understand the appeal of something a little bigger."

He nodded and turned to face the rest of the store only to pause. "For the record, I'm also plenty happy with your dick." With that he walked off and I laughed to myself as I freed myself from the harness.

It didn't take long for Camron to find an attachment he liked. At first I thought the pale length was him teasing me about being a vampire. Only to find it was much worse. "It glows in the dark."

"Excuse me?"

"Says so on the box."

"You can't trust marketing like that." The more I looked at it the more I noticed the green undertone of the pale silicone. I rolled my eyes. "Who comes up with these things?"

"Horny people. Really horny people."

"We're buying it, what does that make us?"

"Suckers, I guess."

Credit to the cashier, he made eye contact with us without making it feel awkward. Even asked if we had lube at home, offered to sell us a small bottle. "Great for travel."

"We're all set, thank you." I pulled out my wallet only to catch Cam doing the same. "Let me."

"It was my idea." He spoke with dignity.

"It's my dick. I'll buy it." I pulled out two hundreds, the flash of green always more enticing than plastic cards. The cashier took my money and I successfully outdid Camron, watched him slip his wallet back into his pocket a bit deflated. I rubbed his lower back. "I do make more money than you."

The cashier snorted but coughed to cover up his outburst.

I kept my hand on Camron's thigh the drive back to my cabin, occasionally letting my hand slide up his leg, my fingers dancing across his fly. Even at half-mast his lust was obvious. My fingertips traced the shape. At one point the car drifted onto the shoulder— the cab rumbled and Camron cursed under his breath before correcting the wheel.

It was a mad dash inside, Camron flinging himself into the shower. Alone with the leather and silicone I found myself suddenly self conscious. What should I wear beneath the straps I wondered? Cursing myself for not buying some cheap, lacy briefs as well. Though I held doubt that would have been very comfortable. My average briefs would have to do— and in the end it didn't much matter.

The toy felt nice between my legs, this pale green thing that was nowhere near anatomical immediately felt a part of me. While lectures of neurons, subjective embodiment, and the cleverness of the brain came to mind, I chose to ignore that in favor of what felt right. This was an extension of me. A part of me that had always been there, just not quite the same shape.

And mine certainly didn't glow. I shut off the light to check if the claim was true just as Camron walked in wearing a towel around his waist. "Oh wow." To our delight the toy glowed a faint green like a stick-on star I'd seen in pediatric wings. "Not sure this is my kink but it's fun."

I scoffed and turned the light back on. "You picked it." I marched over and pulled the towel from his waist. Camron just looked down at me with a dreamy expression. I began stroking his cock and his eyes closed, my touch pulled slow breaths from his lips.

"Your dick could shoot fireworks and I'd still love it, baby." I hardly even needed to touch him, his cock quick to become hard and bounce against his stomach. He went to the bed and I grabbed the lube, snapping it open but not yet pouring any on my fingers.

Instead I got on my knees and brought my mouth to his hole, kissing it before my tongue made contact. Camron's body tensed against my tongue. "Relax." My voice rumbled against the curve of his ass. "Take a breath, love."

I heard him take a deep breath and watched his body relax. "Talk to me while I get you ready." I commanded, always having loved his dirty talk. My tongue returned to his hole, circling it lazily.

"You always surprise me…" he panted. "So fucking filthy." I pressed my tongue inside him and to my delight he was loose enough to let me pass. Though his voice caught in his throat. "You treat me so well, Levi. No one else— *fuck*—" His head bowed before gasping, "only in dreams could anyone fuck me just right— just like you do."

I poured the lube onto my fingers, pulled my face back so I could speak. "It's good you know that, dearest." I slipped a finger inside him and he whimpered. My attempts at being stern like the dominants I'd seen in basements faltered. "I never thought I could have you like this." Another finger in his hole. "But you're so eager."

"I've wanted you for so long Levi."

"And you'll have me. For as long as you live Camron, you have me."

My own impatience caused me to pull my fingers out so I could focus on getting the toy ready, slathering the head and shaft with lube. Still stroking myself I stood back up, Cameron lifting his head to watch me. "Have you done this before?" I should have asked sooner but he'd been so keen on me topping him I just assumed he had.

To my relief he nodded. "It's been a while, but I'll know if it's too much." A crooked smirk tugged at his lips. "You're just so *big* Levi."

I pressed the head of my cock inside him and his thighs shivered. Taking a second to admire the sight of me inside him, I paused to make eye contact, make sure he was still alright. Camron's eyes had never seemed so bright. Not even when he was a werewolf. Again, I looked down to take in the sight of my length slipping inside him.

Camron whimpered, his lip trembling. "It *has* been a while," I taunted. "You're a mess already."

"Darlin' I am always a mess for you."

Our lips met, then our hips as I thrust into him. He kept his legs apart while I bucked forward and back. My fingers scraped along his stomach and chest, appreciating his hair and heft as I always did. He pulled away to say to me, "You're heaven Levi. Or maybe hell— fuck I can't think."

Hand sliding down his body I reached his dick and touched its tip, chuckling when a bead of cum gathered on my fingertip. I paused my thrusting, stopping fully sheathed inside him, and brought my fingertip to my tongue. The salty taste was welcome, such a concentrated single flavor unlike blood.

"Now what do you think?" I asked as I took hold of the base of his dick.

"That I'd give up anything for you to make me cum right now..."

"Lay back down."

Camron leaned back onto the bed and I followed, taking his pec in my mouth. There was just enough room for my arm to rest on his stomach as I stroked his length. Rutted my hips against him. I listened closely, waiting for the short sharp breaks he would take before his final gasp, his *petite mort*. Just as I felt his muscles tense and a groan echoed in his throat I bit down. My fangs pierced his pec and blood filled my mouth.

"Levi!" I heard the ripping of sheets. Caught a glimpse of his bawled fists gripping torn fabric, the bare mattress exposed. He spilled onto my hand and whimpered as I fed from him. My hand kept moving, slower now, making sure every drop of his lust was spent. Gorging myself on the rich taste of his blood. When he started squirming like he was uncomfortable, I released his length. Lapped at his wound till it closed and finally, pulled out.

"Too much?"

Camron rubbed his stomach. "Fuck me, Levi.

"Well..." I pursed my lips almost stopping myself. "I just did."

"Come here and hold me."

I obliged, my hand still dripping with cum and the strap still heavy between my legs. My soaked hand hung awkwardly between us before Camron offered me a piece of the torn sheet. Now clean I wrapped my arms around him and he melted into my embrace. We lay there, our legs dangling off the edge of the bed.

"Do you really not remember the night you were turned?" We were resting on pillows then. My strap lay on the bedside table. The fitted sheet was still ripped but neither of us had enough energy to change it out. Well, I had the energy, the rush of fucking Camron and drinking his blood made me wired. But I'd be damned if I made Camron stand up.

His eyes were half lidded as they had been since we finished fucking. "I remember its eyes..." He nuzzled into my neck. "They were so bright, worse than LED headlights. Probably because they had a soul behind them or something... I don't remember anything else. Just the eyes. The banging in my chest. Feeling like prey and then... It was morning."

I brought my nose to his crown, losing myself in his dirty blond hair.

"When I was traveling out west, a stranger approached our camp. My companions shouted at him to leave. Couldn't spare any of our rations but I insisted he stay. Just get warm by the fire since he looked so damn pale and worn. I slept. Woke up and thought my bedroll must have caught fire... But the heat was inside me, caught in my throat and I had to quench it—" I bit on my tongue.

Camron stirred, moving so we were eye to eye. "You ever told anyone that story?"

I shook my head.

"Figured... never told anyone mine either. Haven't told you about my first full moon yet either."

My jaw relaxed and tongue felt numb but of course it could not bleed. I cupped his cheek and told him without a word I would listen when he was ready.

ON A CLOUDLESS NIGHT, the moon illuminated the woods in pure white light. I sat on a branch at the top of a tree, admiring that meteorite. The same moon I'd admired as a child. Moonlight was the closest I'd ever get to sunlight ever again. It wasn't so bad. At least it was peaceful in the dark, just me and Camron.

Even from the treetop I heard a low growl down below. I slid off the branch, floating down. Camron's glowing eyes greeted me, then his claws as he reached up to catch me. He wrapped his arms around my legs, effectively making a new perch for me to sit on.

I admired him, same as I admired the moon. His long snout, his dark brown fur that covered him head to toe, his wide ears... He bared his teeth, sharp and yellowed. I just bent down to kiss his black nose.

We were the only two people in the world who could see each other for ourselves. Even on that inevitable day that I'm alone, I'll cherish that fact: Camron Coinin knew me and he loved me.

Acknowledgments

A special thank you to everyone who read A Doctor's Touch as a newsletter magnet. The support means the world.

Thank you to Elle Porter and TK Jameson for beta reading and for always supporting horny antics.

To Miranda Sapphire who gave A Doctor's Touch the love it needed and providing copy editing services, it's the care and support like this that makes indie publishing so gratifying.

All the love to Jasmine Garcia who fawned over this story, another instance of just how warm the indie author community is.

Ram Skin Series

A Doctor's Touch

Peaceful in the Dark

About the Author

Arin was born and raised along the American east coast and has called the city, the shore, and the country their home. They've come a long way from writing anime fanfiction in their bedroom and even have a BA in creative writing. When they're not writing Arin enjoys playing tabletop games, drinking coffee, and collecting bits and bobbles. They currently live in Stephen King's backyard with their partner, cat, and lizard.

www.ingramcontent.com/pod-product-compliance
Lightning Source LLC
Chambersburg PA
CBHW061637130726
47996CB00003B/1325